The
Case
of the
Blue
Raccoon

James Heneghan

**Cover by
Janet Wilson**

Scholastic Canada Ltd

Scholastic Canada Ltd.
123 Newkirk Road, Richmond Hill, Ontario, Canada L4C 3G5
Scholastic Inc.
555 Broadway, New York, NY 10012, USA
Scholastic Australia Pty Limited
PO Box 579, Gosford, NSW 2250, Australia
Scholastic New Zealand Limited
Private Bag 94407, Greenmount, Auckland, New Zealand
Scholastic Publications Ltd.
Villiers House, Clarendon Avenue, Leamington Spa,
Warwickshire CV32 5PR, UK

Canadian Cataloguing in Publication Data

Heneghan, James, 1930-
  The case of the blue raccoon

ISBN 0-590-24934-7

I. Title.

PS8565.E581C37 1996   jC813'.54   C96-930236-3
PZ7.H35Ca 1996

6 5 4 3 2 1   Printed in Canada   6 7 8 9 /9
                Manufactured by Webcom Limited

SCHOLASTIC BOOKS
BY JAMES HENEGHAN

The O'Brien Detective Agency Series:

The Case of theMarmalade Cat

The Trail of the Chocolate Thief

The Mystery of the Gold Ring

The Case of the Blue Raccoon

Goodbye, Carlton High

(with Bruce McBay, as B.J. Bond)

Blue

For Margaux Seeley and Lee Cannon-Brown.

With grateful thanks for assistance to
Joseph J. Frederick, Capilano Pest Control;
Mike McIntosh, Vancouver Park Board;
and the staff of
B.C. Fish and Wildlife Management,
Lower Mainland Region.

Chapter 1

The three members of the O'Brien Detective Agency zoomed down Fairview Slopes to False Creek on their bicycles. Then they raced along the seawall and across the tiny wooden bridge onto Granville Island.

It was Friday morning, the beginning of the Easter weekend. The three detectives were on their way to Granville Market for fudge. They were in a hurry. They swooped between the Waterfront Theatre and Kids Only Market, rattled along the boardwalk at Brokers Bay, pedalled furiously past the sailboats and motor cruisers, zigzagged through the boat yard, and came to an abrupt stop among the fluttering, indignant pigeons outside the market.

They parked their bicycles in the rack.

"Chocolate ripple fudge," murmured Brick, a skinny boy with spiky yellow hair.

"Butterscotch," said Sadie Stewart, a slight girl with long brown hair and glasses.

"Maple fudge for me," said Clarice O'Brien, red-haired Chief Detective.

They plunged into the market.

The owner of the fudge shop was a large man with a red face and a tall white hat. When he saw the three detectives approaching he quickly whipped away the tray of free samples from the counter top.

"Did you see what he did?" muttered Clarice.

"He always does that." Sadie had noticed this many times before. The fudge man, joking and jolly with his adult customers, was mean to children, scowling at them and removing his free samples from their eager fingers.

"Good morning," said Sadie politely.

"What do you want?" growled the fudge man.

"Butterscotch fudge, two dollars' worth please," said Sadie.

"Don't lean on the counter," said the fudge man. "Can't you see it's glass?"

The fudge man's assistant served them, a thin young woman with glasses and a sad face.

"Thanks very much," said Clarice, the last to be served.

The detectives took their purchases outside into the spring sunshine and sat on a bench.

A fresh breeze tumbled in from Georgia Strait, danced down Burrard Inlet, curled around the pots of hyacinths set in boxes outside the market, and tangled the girls' hair, especially Sadie's, which moved even when she walked. The three detectives chewed their candy and listened to a man playing a flute.

"I wonder why the fudge man is such a sour-puss?" said Clarice.

Sadie shrugged. "Some people are just naturally mean. Born that way, I expect."

They chewed in silence, listening to the music.

The flutist was tall and thin, with a receding chin and narrow shoulders. He had a merry face. He was dressed in a long coat, the right side of which was red, and the left yellow. His brightly coloured hat sported a long peacock feather that tossed about in the air above him as he played. His eyes were a bright, piercing blue and they twinkled in the sunshine. Although the day was warm and sunny, the piper wore a long red-and-yellow scarf that matched his coat. At his feet there was a bowl for coins. His music was hauntingly melodic and penetrating.

Clarice said, "Makes me feel like dancing."

"He's like the Pied Piper," said Sadie.

"What do you mean?" said Clarice.

The hyacinth-scented breeze blew Sadie's brown hair rebelliously about her face. " 'The Pied Piper of Hamelin' is a famous poem by Robert Browning. *Everybody* knows it, Clarice," she said pompously. "Would you like me to tell the story?"

"No, thanks."

"A strange piper comes to town wearing a red-and-yellow outfit just like that one." Sadie jerked her chin at the market piper. "And he charms animals into following him. He gets rid of a whole plague of rats by drowning them in the river."

Though a year younger than her two friends, Sadie read a lot, and when she wasn't busy helping solve a crime, usually had her nose stuck in a book. Crammed full of information, Sadie was a walking hundred-gigabyte database.

"Rats," murmured Brick, staring at the ends of the pied piper's scarf tossing and fluttering in the breeze. He gazed unblinkingly, like a cat watching a bird in the garden. He seemed fascinated by the piper.

With his strange amber eyes under their yellow lashes, and his freckles the same colour as his eyes, Brick had a sun-baked, tawny look to him. If you wanted to paint him, all you'd need would be yellows and golds.

Clarice laughed. "Look, the pied piper is charming a pair of cats."

The two cats, one white and the other ginger, were sitting together in the shade with their whiskers pointed attentively toward the piper.

Sadie's mouth dropped open. "He's the real Pied Piper, same as the one in the poem! He can charm the animals!"

Clarice said, "Oh sure! And when he gets enough of them he'll drown them in False Creek!"

Sadie scowled. "No need to scoff, Clarice. You'd better be careful. The townspeople in the poem scoffed at the Pied Piper and refused to pay him for getting rid of the rats, so you know what he did? He played his pipe again and charmed all the children into following him. The whole town of Hamelin was emptied of kids."

"What happened to them?" asked Clarice.

"Nobody knows. They just disappeared."

"And never came back?"

Sadie nodded. "Disappeared forever."

"Hmmph!" said Clarice. "It's just a made-up story."

"No it isn't," said Sadie. "It really happened."

A flock of Canada geese flew overhead, honking, it seemed to Sadie, at the piper.

Clarice turned to Brick. "Do all animals like music, Number Three?"

Brick did not answer. His eyes were fixed on the piper.

Brick seldom spoke. His main usefulness as a detective was his astonishing athletic ability, for when it came to climbing rooftops and squeezing through windows he was worth his weight in chocolate ripple fudge.

"Look over there by the garbage!" said Sadie, pointing. "It's a skunk!"

A glossy black skunk, his white-tipped tail

curled behind him, was slouching around the garbage bins opposite Blackberry Books, about half a block away.

"It's very unusual for nocturnal animals to be out so early in the morning," said Sadie, her voice full of awe.

"What's 'knock turner'?" said Clarice.

"Nocturnals sleep in the day and come out at night. Skunks and raccoons are nocturnal. Owls and bats too. You know what I think, Clarice?"

"What?"

"I think the piper's music brought the cats and the skunk here."

"Hmmph!" said Clarice, pushing her half-empty fudge bag into her jacket pocket. "Let's get out of here before that skunk squirts his stinko all over us. Maybe there's a Case waiting for us to solve back at Headquarters." When talking about detective work, Clarice often spoke in capitals.

Sadie followed Clarice, pushing her bicycle. She looked around for Brick, but he was still staring, mesmerized, at the piper. Sadie went back and shook him. "Number Three?" She tapped on the top of his spiky yellow head. "Anyone home?"

Brick got up, grabbed his bicycle, and followed reluctantly after the girls. Before they left, Sadie dropped a couple of nickels into the pied piper's bowl. She looked around for the skunk but it had disappeared. She mounted her bicycle and followed her two friends, pushing her way up the Fairview Slopes.

When they got to Sixth Avenue they turned into the back lane, swooped through the open gate, and parked their bicycles against the potting shed in Clarice's backyard. The shed was their headquarters. The sign on the outside of the shed said:

O'BRIEN DETECTIVE AGENCY
NO JOB TOO BIG OR TOO SMALL
CLARICE O'BRIEN, Chief Detective

The sign could be seen clearly by anyone passing in the back lane.

Clarice checked the coffee tin nailed on the door for messages. There was none. Clarice and Sadie sat at the desk under the window, Clarice in the chair that had CHIEF DETECTIVE painted on the back in white, and Sadie in the chair normally used to seat clients, at the side of the desk, near the door. Brick sprawled himself out, not on the top of the sacks of seed potatoes where he usually lay, for Mr. O'Brien had planted them all, but on a square of thin plywood and a small heap of empty hessian sacks which now occupied the same space. He stretched his arms and legs, scratched his chest, yawned, and closed his eyes.

Sadie intended to have a quiet read while combing out the snarls the wind had made of her hair. She had just pulled *Mammals of the Woodland* from her jacket pocket when there came a loud, assertive knock on the door. She opened it. A little girl with black hair in a braid and bright black eyes waited impatiently outside.

"Yes?" said Sadie.

"You've got to help me!" said the girl wildly. "A terrible crime has been committed!"

Chapter 2

"Crime?" said Sadie to the little girl. "What kind of crime?"

"Somebody stole my rabbit," said the girl.

"We don't do rabbits," said Sadie.

The girl's face fell. She looked as if she were about to cry.

"We only solve real crimes," said Sadie, unmoved by the girl's display of grief. "Lost rabbits are not real crimes, sorry." She tried to close the door but the girl had her foot in it.

" 'No job too big or too small,' " quoted the girl who, it seemed, was not about to cry at all. "It's right there on your sign, take a look." She jerked a thumb at the sign on the outside of the shed, glared at Sadie, and stuck out her lower lip in a challenging way.

"Let her in, Number Two," said Clarice.

The girl marched in. She noticed Brick asleep on the floor. "What's the matter with him?"

"That's Number Three," said Sadie. "He was up all night trying to remember his name."

"Take no notice of Sadie," Clarice said to the girl. "Number Three just likes to relax in between exhausting criminal cases. Crime Fighting isn't easy. Being a Detective can be dirty and it can be tough. He gets drained emotionally. What's your name?"

"Shivon Silva."

"What's your rabbit's name?"

"Betsy Bunny. She was stoled from my backyard."

"Take that down, Number Two," Clarice said to Sadie.

Sadie was secretary as well as Detective Number Two. But she made no attempt to reach across the desk for her notebook and one of the sharp pencils standing in a mug. Instead, she rolled her eyes at the ceiling, then gazed longingly at her book, which she'd left on the seat of the client chair.

"Was Betsy in a rabbit hutch?" said Clarice.

"No. She just lives in the backyard nibbling on grass and buttercups."

"There aren't any buttercups out yet."

"She's been making do with those little white daisies."

"What does Betsy look like?"

"Well, she's very cuddly and soft, and she's black 'n' white, and she's very gentle, and she's got a quivery nose and 'normous long ears." Shivon held her hands out to indicate their length.

Sadie reached across the desk and made a show of grabbing the notebook and a pencil. "Long ears?" she said in mock astonishment. "That must be very unusual on a rabbit — long ears, I mean you usually see such tiny ones, don't you, on a rabbit? I'd better be sure to write that down." She made an elaborate performance of writing in the notebook: "Betsy Rabbit has ENORMOUS LONG EARS."

Sadie could be very sarcastic.

Clarice gave Sadie a dark look, then turned her attention back to Shivon. "How do you know Betsy didn't run away? Or wander off? She could be in the next yard."

"She was stoled last night. I heard noises in the back lane a few minutes after I'd gone to bed, so I looked out the window and saw a man lifting a big heavy cage into the back of a van. I couldn't see too clear, but I know there was animals in the cage."

"What animals?"

"I dunno."

"Did you see Betsy in the cage?"

"No. But this morning when I looked, Betsy was gone." Shivon's face crumpled again.

Clarice spoke quickly. "Was the van parked near your house?"

Shivon shook her head. No tears, just anger. "It was right next door, outside Mrs. Reardon's."

"Sadie — Number Two — will take down your address and Mrs. Reardon's," said Clarice. "Also, we'll need a description of the van. We'll come by later to take a look at your backyard."

"How much do you charge?" asked Shivon.

"For a rabbit?" Clarice scratched her red head. "Three chocolate bars."

"What kind?"

"Robin Hoods will be fine."

When Shivon had gone, Sadie tossed note-book and pencil contemptuously onto the desk.

"What a total waste of time. Stolen rabbit! Good grief!"

"No job too small," Clarice reminded her. "A Lost Rabbit Case is better than no Case. Besides, I've got a Hutch this will turn out to be . . . interesting."

"Hunch."

"Huh?"

"You've got a *hunch*."

"That's what I said, Hunch."

Clarice believed she was the possessor of a powerful sixth sense that provided her with special insights unavailable to the rest of humanity. She called these insights "Hunches."

"Wake Number Three up," said Clarice, "and let's go check the Scene of the Crime."

Chapter 3

"Well, there's no long-eared Easter bunny around here," said Sadie, taking off her glasses and wiping them with a small square of soft cloth she always carried in her jacket pocket for that purpose.

Their search of the backyards on Shivon's block had revealed no rabbits, only sleeping cats and bad-tempered watchdogs.

"Let's go talk to the lady next door, Mrs. Reardon," said Clarice. "Maybe she can tell us something about the man with the cage. Which house is it?"

Sadie consulted her notebook. "That one." She pointed.

Clarice called up to Brick who was hanging onto the chimney on Shivon's roof. "Number Three!"

Brick was shading his eyes against the sun as he gazed about the landscape for a glimpse of rabbit. "Right, Chief," he said. He sat, slid down the roof, twisted, and came down the drainpipe like a monkey, landing lightly on the ground in a crouch. Then he leaped, kicked one foot into the air, and whirled smartly, adroitly missing the downspout. Both hands chopped the air like knives. "Harrraaah!" he yelled.

Mrs. Reardon's house, like the others on the block, was an old two-storey with clapboard siding and several steps up from the street to a wide front porch. Today the porch was carpeted with pink-and-purple petals blown in from the huge magnolia tree in the front yard. A child's rocking chair which someone had been painting blue was perched on the porch railing to dry, and underneath it on the deck was the pot of paint. A few magnolia petals clung to the sticky paint on the lid of the tin.

Clarice twisted the reluctant, old-fashioned bell on the front door. An old lady poked her head out of an open window on the first floor. "Yes?"

"Mrs. Reardon?" said Clarice.

"Yes?"

"Do you know anything about a man with animal cages? He was parked outside your house last night, in the back lane."

"That'd be the pest control man. Why?"

"We're looking for—"

"I can't hear you," said Mrs. Reardon. "Wait there."

She came to the door and peered at the three detectives through her wire-frame glasses. "Now what is it?"

With the sleeve of her jacket, Clarice wiped a smear of maple fudge off the corner of one of the new cards they'd had printed and handed it to the old lady. The card said O'BRIEN DETECTIVE AGENCY, and had their three names, Clarice's address and telephone number, and a fingerprint seen through a magnifying glass. "I'm Clarice and this is Sadie and this is Brick. We're detectives and we're looking for a rabbit who disappeared from Shivon Silva's house next door. Have you seen it?"

"You must mean Betsy. No. I didn't know Shivon had lost her. What a shame. I often fed her lettuce leaves through the fence — Betsy, I

mean, not Shivon. Friendly little thing —
Shivon, that is. But I'm not surprised really with
all the raccoons about this year — seems like
they had a population explosion. The raccoons
probably got the poor little thing. Betsy, not
Shivon of course." She gave a little laugh.

Sadie said, "Got? You mean—"

Mrs. Reardon nodded deliberately. "Got."

Clarice said, "Is that why the pest control
man was here? To trap raccoons?"

Mrs. Reardon nodded again. "I've never
seen so many raccoons and skunks as I've seen
this year. They're everywhere. I reckon it's all
the mild winters we've been having these last
few years. Raccoons are the worst. There was
a family living under my porch, raccoons that
is. My own fault of course. All through the
winter I fed the mother scraps on the porch
right there where you're standing, and then
before long there were six of them! The mother
had five babies! She came scratching and snuf-
fling outside my door every night driving me
strawberries. So I had the pest man come and
take them away."

Sadie's face was pale. "Did he kill them?"

Mrs. Reardon shook her head so hard her

grey hair danced about her face. "Goodness me, no!"

Sadie breathed a sigh of relief.

Mrs. Reardon smiled. "He said he would take them far away and release them into the wilderness."

"Do you think he might have taken Shivon's pet rabbit by mistake?" said Clarice.

"Shouldn't think so, my dear."

"You think the raccoons ate Betsy, don't you, Mrs. Reardon?" said Sadie.

The old lady's mouth puckered sympathetically. "A hungry raccoon is worse than a tiger. I told Shivon she'd be better keeping Betsy in a proper hutch instead of letting her roam about the yard. I'm only surprised a raccoon or an eagle didn't get her sooner. Or one of the dogs. There are lots of dogs in the neighbourhood. There's a Doberman on the opposite side of the street, for instance, that I wouldn't want to meet on a dark night. He looks at me with—"

"Thanks, Mrs. Reardon," said Clarice, straddling her bicycle and pushing off along the sidewalk. Sadie and Brick followed her along the street and into the lane behind Shivon's house. Clarice dismounted.

"Why are we stopping?" asked Sadie.

"We didn't check Shivon's backyard for evidence of murder."

"Murder?" said Sadie.

Clarice climbed over the fence into the yard. "If a raccoon or a dog or eagle killed Betsy then it's a Murder. There should be signs of a struggle, and blood and fur in the grass where the killing took place. Search every square centimetre."

They searched. They found no blood or fur or any evidence of a struggle to the death.

"What if the killer dragged the body to a different location and ate it there?" said Sadie. "The Doberman across the street, maybe?"

"We can't search everyone's yard," said Clarice. "Besides, I'm hungry."

They free-wheeled lazily down the hill to Granville Island and parked their bicycles outside the market. They bought fruit from the Chinese lady's fruit stand and pop from the machine outside the market, then sat eating and drinking and idly watching the boats come and go in the marina. Hyacinths still scented the air, and over on the other side of False Creek the late afternoon sunshine glinted off the tops of downtown highrise condominiums and office towers.

"What do you think, Clarice?" said Sadie. "Was Betsy bunnyburger?"

"Impossible to say. But if Betsy was butchered then it wasn't in her own backyard."

They sipped and chewed in silence. Then Clarice said, "Betsy is black and white."

"Was black and white," said Sadie.

"Shivon said it was getting dark, remember?" said Clarice. "Maybe Mrs. Reardon is wrong and the pest man really did mistake Betsy for a raccoon and took her away in a cage."

They swigged for a while in silence.

Sadie said, "You know what I think? I think Betsy heard the pied piper's music and hippity-hopped down Fairview Slopes to Granville Island."

"Hippity-hopped?"

"Hippity-hopped, *lured* by the music."

The way Sadie dragged out *lured* hinted of dark and mysterious forces totally beyond human understanding.

Clarice sighed impatiently. "Why would the pied piper want to *lure* an old rabbit? Makes no sense."

"I don't know," admitted Sadie. "Maybe he kidnaps valuable pets and sells them off."

"The trouble with you, Number Two," said Clarice, airily dismissing Sadie's theory with a wave of her hand, "is you read too much. Reading messes up your head, gibbles your eyes and causes cellulose in your brains. Shouldn't be surprised if scientists discover it clogs your arteries with testosterone and fatty acids and stuff like that. Shortens your life, everyone knows that. You use up brain cells trying to read all those tiny words on the page. Anyway, I don't think Betsy could hear as far as Granville Island. It must be at least a kilometre to the market from Shivon's house."

Brick hurled his apple core at a seagull parked on the rail. Then with acrobatic smoothness he jumped onto his bicycle and, without a word to his friends, pedalled off, leaving his empty pop can on the bench. Accustomed to Brick's strange comings and goings, the girls calmly watched his spiky yellow head recede in the distance. Brick, they knew, didn't move to the tick-tock of a regular clock. His sense of time came from some internal rhythm all his own.

"You're wrong about Betsy not hearing, Clarice," said Sadie. "That's why rabbits have such big ears. They have powerful hearing, just

22

like me." Sadie's slightly prominent ears, usually hidden under her long hair but visible now as the wind blew it about, were indeed very sensitive, and had proved useful on many of their cases.

"Isn't that him?" Clarice jerked her chin. "In the coffee shop."

Sadie looked. It *was* the pied piper, seated at a small table, reading a newspaper. His red-and-yellow scarf trailed behind onto the floor. They watched him. After a while he finished his coffee, put on his hat with the long feather, picked up his pipe, and strolled away past the Arts Club Theatre and along the road leading off the island. Sadie became excited. "He's going home! Let's follow him."

"Why?"

"He's the only suspect we have in the missing rabbit case, and besides, I'd like to see where he lives."

"It's getting late, Number Two. We should go home."

"But what if the pied piper has got all these animals in his house, and—and—and he's some kind of an animal kidnapper, and—and—"

Clarice gathered the empty cans together and

dropped them in the recycling bin. "Face the truth, Number Two: the raccoons ate Betsy." She shrugged. "But if it will make you feel any better we can follow him on our bikes just to see where he lives."

They mounted their bicycles and followed a short distance behind the piper as he strolled along the Brokers Bay seawall, past the fishing boats, through the gap in the fence, over the railway tracks, past Molson's Brewery, over a muddy ditch and into Vanier Park, a narrow strip of wilderness between the Vancouver Museum and Granville Island.

The sun was almost down and the light was fading. They had to walk their bicycles along the narrow, overgrown dirt paths, squeezing through thick hawthorne and alder brush noisy with birdsong; ducking their heads under looping arcs of thorny blackberry bushes, tripping over the roots of ferns. Several times they almost lost sight of the piper, but the bright colours of his outfit and the tall, waving hat feather helped keep him in view. Then they came to a clump of trees and stopped. They looked about them. The piper had disappeared.

"Where did he go?" whispered Clarice.

Sadie pointed to a tall hemlock tree, thick with leafy branches and noisy with the excited evening chatter of birds. "I think he's sitting under the tree," she whispered.

They left their bicycles on the ferny ground and crept toward the tree.

Music. They stopped and looked at each other with raised eyebrows.

The piper was sitting on the ground with his back against the tree, playing his flute. The sound came out sweet and clear and the birdsong rose louder and louder, blending with the high piping flute into an orchestra of harmonic sounds.

They stood for a while, listening, captured by the sounds, then Clarice pulled Sadie away and they returned to their bicycles. "It'll be dark soon, Sadie, so let's go."

Sadie sighed. "Clarice, pipe music in the woods at sunset — it's so beautiful!" She sighed again. "Let's wait a little longer and listen. Then we can see where he goes."

"I don't care where he goes." Clarice lifted her bicycle off the ground. Then she stopped. "What the—!"

Sadie followed the direction of her gaze.

White stripe and thick black fur.

"It's Betsy!" said Sadie, dropping her bicycle and springing forward.

Clarice stared, horrified. "Stop! It's a skunk!"

Sadie stopped.

She was so scared she was unable to move.

The skunk, surprised and alarmed by Sadie's attack, began hissing and stamping its feet threateningly, its bushy, white-tipped tail bristling high in the air.

Sadie screamed, "He's going to spray!"

"Run for it!" yelled Clarice.

But it was too late. The skunk, already curled and folded into a U-shaped rocket launcher, its tail in the air and its pointed nose and back end both aimed at them, fired a salvo of musk that enveloped the two girls in a fine penetrating spray.

"Eeeeh!" screamed Sadie as the deadly acrid stink made her gag.

"Arrrgh!" yelled Clarice.

The skunk slunk away.

Someone was laughing.

The pied piper.

Sadie, her eyes watering and stinging, could dimly see him: he was holding his nose with one hand and waving goodbye with the other as he hurried away along the trail through the trees, heading toward the museum parking lot.

The girls grabbed their bicycles and ran blindly, tripping and stumbling in the opposite direction through the lush greenery, the sounds of the birds and the piper's laughter screaming in their ears.

Chapter 4

The sun was shining as Sadie pedalled hotly up the Fairview Slopes. She was definitely not feeling her best; her skin felt prickly all over from yesterday's scrubbing and her head hurt. With her hair hanging limp and lifeless about her ears and her eyes red-rimmed and dull, she looked a sight and she knew it. Which was why she was hiding her face under a baseball cap, its peak pulled down to the rims of her glasses.

There was no breeze this Saturday morning and the air was heavy with the scent of horse chestnut and mountain ash blossoms, and the gardens, and hedges shone with yellow laburnum, pink azalea and scarlet japonica. Cheerful and bright. Except that Sadie did not feel cheerful and bright. Miserable and dull would be more like it.

She was carrying, on the handlebars of her bicycle, a plastic Safeway bag stuffed with borrowed clothing, and was wearing one of her old jackets. It was a faded red, the zipper was broken and it was a bit small for her in the sleeves. Sadie's back was sweating, which made the prickly feeling worse. She thought about stopping to take off the jacket, but that would mean having to lose momentum on the hill. She kept going.

Perspiring and out of breath, she arrived at headquarters to find Clarice telling Brick all the awful details of their encounter with the skunk.

Brick was grinning.

"Here she comes," said Clarice. "Here's Detective Number Two, now demoted to Detective Number Zero on account of her totally stupid theory about a pied piper kidnapping a rabbit."

Clarice looked terrible: her beautiful red hair, normally shiny, was limp and dull, her eyes were almost as red as her hair and her complexion was puffy and mottled.

Sadie's face fell. "Demoted?"

"You got it, Number Zero!" said Clarice. "Demoted!"

Sadie collapsed into the chair beside the desk. "But that's not fair, Clarice. It wasn't my fault the skunk sprayed us."

"Oh no? Then who charged at it like a starving sumo wrestler spotting a plate of sushi?"

Brick, activated perhaps by the thought of wrestling, leaped to his feet and high-kicked the potting shed roof. "Aaaah!" he shrieked, arms whirling.

"Cool it, Number Three," said Clarice.

Brick sat on the floor and quietly folded himself into a pretzel shape.

"So, we came back here," Clarice continued to Brick, "and my dad burned all our clothes, and my mom made us sit in the bathtub for an hour and scrub all over with ammonia and tomato juice! I can still smell that dirty skunk on me! Can't get the stink of skunk and ammonia out of my hair and my skin and my fingernails!"

Brick grinned.

"It's not funny!" said Sadie, almost crying. "Clarice, you can't demote me, you just can't!"

"I hope you brought back my jeans and sweater," Clarice said coldly.

Sadie threw the plastic Safeway bag of clothing onto the desk. "You can keep your old clothes. And you can keep your stupid detective job too! I've had enough! I don't want to be a detective any more. I try really hard to be a good detective and what do I get? Demotion! The charter of human rights is on my side, Clarice, and—and you won't get away with this—and—and—" She burst into tears and fled out the door.

Clarice had gone too far. She jumped to her feet. "Sadie! Come back!"

Sadie stopped while she fumbled in her old jacket pocket for a tissue.

"Cool it, Number Two. There's no need to get so upset."

"Number Two?" Sadie sniffed. "I'm still Number Two? I'm not demoted?"

"Come back inside. No, you're not demoted. But the pied piper's got nothing to do with this Case, so forget him, okay? Betsy was either eaten by some other animal or . . . " Clarice plunged back into the shed.

Sadie found a crumpled paper napkin and followed her, drying her eyes and blowing her nose.

Clarice became businesslike. " . . . or there is

some other explanation. My powerful Sixth Sense tells me to follow a Hunch. It means that we don't sit in the office waiting for clues to walk in, we get out there and give it some good old Legwork. Today we check out the pest man." She looked sternly at her two helpers. "There's a remote possibility that the pest person took Betsy along with Mrs. Reardon's raccoons by mistake. Any questions?"

Sadie, still sniffling a little, said, "We don't know who the pest person is. Mrs. Reardon didn't tell us his name."

Clarice led the way out the door. "Then our first stop is Mrs. Reardon's."

They leaped onto their bicycles. Brick was first out the gate, whooping and swooping down the bumpy back lane, handlebars on automatic, open hands practice-chopping the lush new growth bursting out at him from backyard fences on either side. The lane was sweet with the perfume of creamy rowan blossoms. Whirling tires kicked up dry dust and gravel. Sadie, still damp from tears and her ride up the hill, pedalled furiously to keep up with her two friends as they tore around the bend and swooped down the hill.

Mrs. Reardon was sweeping magnolia petals from her porch with a whisk broom. She seemed happy to see them, but frowned when she saw the girls' red eyes. "You don't look well, either of you. If I were your mothers I'd put you to bed."

"We're all right," said Clarice. "Could you tell us the name of the pest control person who took your raccoons?"

Mrs. Reardon frowned and looked about her, sniffing. "Can you smell skunk?"

"Skunk cabbage," said Sadie quickly. "The ditches are full of 'em."

"The pest person?" said Clarice.

"The pest person is Patrick Packer. He's at Sixth and Birch. Pied Piper Pest Control he calls himself." Mrs. Reardon's eyes narrowed. "But it wasn't Patrick who did the job; it was his brother Pete. Patrick's off for the weekend. Why do you ask?"

"Pied Piper!" said Sadie, her glasses sliding to the end of her nose in astonishment. She turned to Clarice, her eyes round behind her glasses.

"We want to question him about Betsy," said Clarice, ignoring her friend.

"I'm very annoyed with Mr. Pete Packer," said

Mrs. Reardon angrily. "He took the mother raccoon and only *four* of the babies. Which I discovered only last night. One little one was left behind, crying half the night for its mother. *Patrick* wouldn't do a thing like that."

"Why didn't you ask for Patrick to do the job for you?" said Sadie.

"I just told you: he's got the weekend off. Gone off on one his crazy holidays, I shouldn't be surprised. I tried calling his brother, Pete, this morning for him to come and take the poor little baby to its mother, but he wasn't there."

"Where is the baby right now?" said Sadie.

"Under the porch. It must be hungry, poor wee thing. I left milk near the entrance hole but it won't come out."

Clarice said, "Number Three?"

"Right, Chief." Brick leaped over the rail and landed lightly on the grass below.

Mrs. Reardon hurried out and leaned over the rail. "You all right, boy?"

"Just watch," said Clarice.

Brick crouched near the hole in the bottom boards of the porch. "Chrrhrr!" he called in a low throaty murmur. He waited. "Chrrhrrchrrhrr!" he called again.

A baby raccoon poked his tiny masked face out and sniffed at Brick's tattered sneakers. Then he sniffed Brick's hands. Brick picked him up gently and held him in his hands, a tiny bundle of black shiny fur about the size of two tennis balls.

"Well I never!" said Mrs. Reardon.

"Brick has a way with animals," Clarice explained.

"He's so cute!" said Sadie, stroking the tiny baby's pointed nose gently with her finger. "Let me hold him, Brick."

Brick handed him carefully and gently to Sadie. The little raccoon, when it caught a whiff of Sadie's skin, whined like a human baby and struggled in Sadie's hands, its ringed tail trembling with fear as he fought to get back to Brick.

Brick said, "Chrrhrr." The raccoon immediately relaxed in Sadie's hands. She made him comfortable inside her jacket, fastening the button at the bottom and sliding the baby raccoon around to her hip so he wouldn't fall out past the broken zipper. "The little baby wascal want his momma?" she murmured into the jacket. "I'll call him Rascal," she said to Clarice, "same as the one in the book."

"Pete Packer must take the poor thing to its mother right away," said Mrs. Reardon firmly.

"We're going over there. We can take Rascal to Mr. Packer's place for you," said Clarice. "It's no trouble."

Mrs. Reardon smiled. "Thank you, children."

Chapter 5

Because of her broken zipper, Sadie rode her bicycle one-handed to the Pied Piper Pest Control shop, keeping the other hand over the bulge in her jacket.

"Clarice," said Sadie, "don't you think there's something fishy about there being two pied pipers, the one on Granville Island and this pest control company?"

"Not really. Granville Island has lots of funny characters. There's the balloon man all dressed up in coloured rags and balloons, and there's the guy dressed up as a clown with all those bird toys that fly, and that's not even mentioning all the funny-looking musicians—"

"Clarice, I'm not talking about—"

"Hear me out, Number Two. Finally, the name Pied Piper, from what you say about the famous poem that everyone in the world is s'posed to know about except me, would be a natural name for a pest control business, right, Number Three?"

"Right, Chief."

Sadie rolled her eyes.

The white van outside the shop had red-and-yellow lettering:

PIED PIPER PEST CONTROL LTD
Ministry of Environment Certified
and Licensed
PATRICK PACKER
The Pest Man

A man sat behind an untidy desk with a telephone clamped between chin and shoulder as he scribbled notes. The desk was cluttered with books, leaflets and brochures. He waved the three detectives to a dusty sofa that had stuffing sticking out in several places. They sat down. Rascal poked his nose out to sniff the rancid air. Sadie thought the place smelled like cockroach powder, a smell even more unpleasant than ammonia. She hoped Rascal wouldn't use her jacket as a bathroom.

She looked around the shop. There was a cage on the floor with a grey squirrel crouching timidly in one of its corners. There were empty wire cages of all sizes stacked against the back wall. The other walls were almost completely covered in posters with pictures and information on rats, mice, fleas, silverfish, caterpillars, moths, skunks, squirrels, beetles, raccoons and a host of other animals.

Sadie turned her head. Behind her hung a notice headed:

MINISTRY of the ENVIRONMENT
REGULATIONS for the LIVETRAPPING
of NUISANCE WILDLIFE SPECIES.

Brick got up and squatted on the floor beside the caged squirrel. He made a few low squeaking sounds. The squirrel squeaked back at him.

The man hung up the phone.

"Are you Mr. Packer?" said Clarice.

"That's me, Pete Packer the pest man. What can I do for you, kids?" He peered at Clarice and

Sadie closely with piercing blue eyes. "You two got the measles or something?" He grinned, revealing long stained teeth with gaps between them like a garden rake. He had a sneering face and a chin like a rat's, which was no chin at all, and what little hair he had was grey and wispy. He needed a shave.

There was something familiar about him; Sadie wondered if she'd seen him somewhere before.

Clarice ignored his rude question and introduced her friends. She flashed her ID card. "We're looking for a black-and-white rabbit named Betsy. She disappeared from 585 West Fifth and we wondered if you could've taken her by mistake when you took Mrs. Reardon's raccoons."

Pete pondered. Then he said, "I never mistake cats for rats, bees for fleas, bugs for slugs, and I never, never mistake rabbits for 'coons."

"So the answer is no?" said Sadie sarcastically.

Brick, bored, had started doing his exercises near the stacked cages, bouncing and marching on the spot, lifting his knees up high toward his chin and making little grunts. As Pete talked to the girls he watched Brick out of the corner of his eye nervously.

"What you got in your jacket, kid?" Pete narrowed his beady little eyes at Sadie.

"You left this little baby behind, separating him from his mother," said Sadie. She opened the top of her jacket revealing Rascal's pointed nose and shiny black eyes.

Pete peered. "Baby 'coon," he said.

Sadie said, "The word is 'raccoon.' It comes from an Algonquian Indian word, *arahkunem*, which means 'he scratches with the hands.' "

"You don't say," said Pete.

Sadie nodded. "I do say. And Mrs. Reardon said you've got to return him to his mother right away."

"Did she now," said Pete, standing and coming out from behind his desk. He was tall and thin, with round shoulders. "Well, I'm busy. It will have to wait." He was wearing soiled jeans and a shapeless old green sweater, dirty and stained, and now that he was closer, Sadie could see that the backs of his hands bore several long scratches or scars that ran from fingers to wrists. She thought she could smell the fear of a thousand animals and bugs on him.

Down at the end of the shop, Brick's exercises

had become more verbal. "Haaarsssh!" he hissed through clenched lips as he attacked the air with feet and elbows.

Pete paled. He backed away as though preparing to flee and sought protection behind his desk. "Your friend seems very violent," he stammered nervously.

"Only when he's awake," said Sadie. She stood and pointed to the poster on the wall behind her. "It says in the Ministry regulations that if you live-trap a nursing female then you've got to take the entire family."

Pete's head was snapping back and forth like a Wimbledon spectator's as he squinted at Brick, then at Sadie, back to Brick, ready to flee behind his desk should Brick decide to attack.

"Entire family," Sadie repeated, trying to get his attention.

Clarice said, "I'm sure you know how much a mother worries when her baby is missing, Mr. Packer. Besides, he's hungry. Couldn't your other business wait?"

"No," said Pete, "it can't wait."

"Then we'll return the baby ourselves," said Clarice, standing. "Just tell us where you took the others."

Pete laughed. "Way up beyond Lions Bay on the Squamish River. Too far for you kids to go."

Clarice frowned. "Why so far?"

"Ministry regulations," said Pete. "Urban raccoons, if they're trapped and moved, got to be let go in the wilderness, in what they call a designated area." He pointed a dirty finger at Rascal. "But there's no way that 'coon could find its mother now." He gave a harsh laugh. "It's been too long. If I left him for his mother to find—" he laughed again. "—an eagle would have his skinny little carcass for supper."

Sadie said, "You could stay with him until his mother came. Raccoons have a strong sense of smell. She would recognize her baby's scent. And she would certainly recognize yours. You're the one who goofed, Mr. Packer. You're responsible."

Pete scowled but said nothing. His fingers made a dry scratching sound on the desk. He seemed to be thinking. "Leave the 'coon with me," he said finally. "I'll take care of it."

Sadie wasn't sure if she could trust Pete to do the job properly. He seemed shifty and deceitful. He simply didn't look like the kind of man who would drive all the way out to the Squamish River just to reunite a baby with its mother.

What if he kept Rascal in one of those awful cages? Or had him killed to save himself the long trip? Sadie made up her mind. "No," she said to Clarice, "let's handle things ourselves." She got up. "Let's go."

Clarice and Brick followed Sadie's straight back and bouncing brown hair out the door.

"I don't think Pete Packer is very dependable," said Sadie when they got outside.

Clarice shrugged. "No, but I believe him when he says he didn't take Betsy. Which leaves only three possibilities. An animal ate her, or she wandered off somewhere, or she was kidnapped. My Hunch is that she wandered off and can't find her way back."

"The pied piper lured her," said Sadie. "Betsy was beguiled and bewitched."

"Or grabbed and gobbled."

"Poor Betsy," said Sadie.

"Looks like you got yourself a baby raccoon, Sadie," said Clarice as they walked their bicycles along Birch.

Sadie was looking down at Rascal inside her jacket. She stopped and leaned her bicycle against the wall. "Take a look at Rascal. Do you think he's all right?"

Clarice and Brick put their faces close to Rascal's. The raccoon's eyes were glazed. He seemed weak.

"Looks a bit dopey," said Clarice. "Maybe it's the skunky ammonia smell on your stinky bod."

"Chrrhrr," said Brick.

The raccoon did not respond.

"Perhaps it's his sleep time," said Sadie anxiously.

"Hungry maybe," said Clarice.

"Taking care of a baby is a big responsibility," said Sadie. "I think I'll take him home and try to feed him." She felt something wet and warm spread around her belly. "Oh, no!" she groaned. "He peed on me!"

Clarice grinned. "I've got to get home too. There's a job I promised my mom I'd do this afternoon." She turned to Brick. "Tomorrow's Sunday. We meet at headquarters, nine sharp."

Chapter 6

The last of the ornamental cherry blossoms glistened on the trees and on the grass verges along Oak Street in the Sunday morning sunshine. Sadie pedalled her mountain bike up the Fairview Slopes with Rascal safely strapped at her waist, inside her mother's fanny pack. She felt better today. Her skin had stopped prickling and her eyes were clear and her mother had sworn that Sadie smelled perfectly normal. No skunk, no ammonia, just the usual sweet Sadie smell, she said.

Sadie felt good. Today she relished the warmth of the sun on her face, the sounds of the bees fumbling in the flowers in neighbourhood gardens, the birds murmuring in the hedges and trees. She zoomed down the back lane into Clarice's yard and parked her bicycle against the shed. Brick's old bike was already there. She was late.

Clarice was at her desk busily tying short lengths of wool and cotton onto cards with holes punched in them and "O'BRIEN YARN COMPANY" printed on the tops. In front of her on the desk were a dozen or so small cardboard boxes containing short lengths of yarns of various thicknesses and colours. She looked better, too. Her hair, dimmed yesterday by the ammonia scrubbing, was back almost to its original fiery red and her eyes were bright green instead of red.

"What are you doing, Clarice?" Sadie asked.

"Helping out," said Clarice. She saw Sadie's puzzled look and explained further. "You know about my mom's mail-order business — yarns and knitting supplies and patterns, all that kind of stuff?"

Sadie nodded.

"And you know about my dad being laid off work?"

Sadie nodded again.

47

"Well, Mom's got him helping with the business now, and they decided to expand. They put ads in a couple of the big magazines and got swamped with orders for catalogues." Clarice waved at the materials on the desk. "So I'm making shade cards to go in the catalogues. My dad says times are hard and we've all got to pull together."

Sadie picked up a completed shade card. Clarice had tied twelve pieces of wool, all different colours, neatly through the twelve punched holes. "Your mom's catalogues have got real wool inside?"

Clarice nodded. "And cotton and silk. Natural fibres. There's about a hundred samples altogether, and they all have to be tied like these."

"Wow!" said Sadie. "Sounds like a lot of work."

Brick, stretched out on the floor as usual, was snoozing. Sadie unzipped her fanny pack, lifted Rascal out carefully and put him on the sacks. The tiny raccoon climbed up onto Brick's skinny belly, curled himself into a ball, and went to sleep.

"Looks like Rascal is okay today," said Clarice.

"He was hungry, that's all. Any clients?"

Clarice, concentrating on threading a piece of red yarn through a hole in a shade card, shook her head.

"Too bad about Betsy," said Sadie. "Do you still think she wandered off? Or that the raccoons had her for dinner?"

Clarice shrugged.

"Do you think we ought to tell Shivon the raccoons might have got her?"

"Better not."

"No, you're right. Probably upset the poor kid. But I still think the pied piper got her, Clarice. I bet Betsy is following him around Granville Island."

Clarice said nothing.

"You must admit, Clarice, the pied piper is pretty weird. I don't like the way he laughed at us when we — you know—"

"I know. I try not to think about it."

"Rascal is so cute. I wish we could keep him."

Clarice said, "So keep him."

"We can't."

"Why not?"

"Because he's a wild animal. He's got to learn to live in the wild. Besides, raccoons are too dangerous to keep. A few months from now he'll have claws and teeth like butcher's knives."

"How do you know so much about raccoons?"

"I read about them. Clarice, did you know that mother raccoons and skunks chase the fathers away as soon as their kittens are born? The mother likes to take care of them all by herself."

"Hmm. Just like people. Mrs. Webster down at the end of the block is like that. Soon after she had her baby she chased her husband out of the house 'cause all he did was sit watching hockey on TV instead of helping."

Sadie crouched and stroked Rascal's soft fur gently with her finger. "I couldn't let Pete Packer take him. I don't think he's a very good pest control person."

"We could let Rascal go," said Clarice. She finished a card and held it up to inspect its twelve different-coloured yarns tied neatly in a row. Then she dropped it into a large cardboard box under the desk.

"He's too little," said Sadie. "Pete Packer's right. Some other animal would eat him — an owl or a hawk or a coyote. He needs his mom till he's old enough to take care of himself."

"We could take him across to Stanley Park,"

said Clarice. She started on a new card. "There's lots of raccoons there. Maybe one would adopt him."

"Hmmn, maybe, but I doubt it. Animals are funny that way. I've read about ewes that refuse to feed any but their own newborn lambs."

"Yeah? So what happens if a ewe dies giving birth but the lamb lives?"

"The farmer forces another ewe to take it, I think."

Clarice worked in silence for a minute. Sadie watched her.

"You could give Rascal to the zoo," said Clarice. "They would know what to do."

"But what if they put him in a cage? Rascal would hate that."

Sadie was itching to feel the brightly coloured yarns in her own fingers, eager to thread them through the holes and tie them expertly with a flip of the fingertips as Clarice was doing.

"Could I help with those cards, Clarice? How do you know which colour to tie through which hole?"

Clarice moved to make room for her at the desk and pointed to a completed card pinned in front of them on the wall underneath the window. "It's easy. Just follow the same colours as the ones in that sample."

Sadie became absorbed in her task. She was a perfectionist, never satisfied until she got things exactly right. Soon she was tying yarns as quickly and as neatly as Clarice, the tip of her tongue visible between her teeth as she concentrated.

Except for Brick's occasional snore, there was complete silence in the potting shed.

By noon the box under the desk was almost full of completed cards. Mrs. O'Brien was very pleased. She brought orange and carrot juice, bagels, tomatoes and cream cheese out to the shed. Brick, smelling the food, was instantly awake. Rascal slid down onto the floor and began squeaking like a kitten.

"He's hungry," said Sadie. She opened her fanny pack and took out a small carton of milk and a straw.

"He can't drink through a straw," said Clarice.

"Oh, really?" said Sadie. "Just watch this." She pushed the straw into the milk, drew a little into her mouth, and then transferred the end of the straw from the milk carton to Rascal's mouth. The baby raccoon sucked on the end of the straw, his black eyes gleaming. Sadie took the straw from her mouth. "This is the way Sterling North fed his baby raccoon in the book."

"What book?" said Clarice.

"The title is *Rascal*. Feeding him this way, with the milk going from my mouth to his, warms the milk so it's more like his own mother's."

Rascal squeaked again. Sadie performed her mother routine many more times before her baby was satisfied. Then she popped the sleepy Rascal into the fanny pack and the three detectives got on their bicycles and sped down the hill to Shivon's house.

Chapter 7

"Did Betsy come home?" asked Clarice.

Shivon pulled a face. "No! That man took her away in a cage, I told you so. 'No job too big or too small!' Hmmph! Some detectives! I don't think you've done a thing about finding Betsy!"

"We questioned Mr. Packer the pest man," said Sadie. "He was the one with the cage."

Shivon's attitude changed. "Yeah?"

Sadie nodded. "He didn't take Betsy."

"Then where could she be?" said Shivon.

"We don't know, but we might have another lead to follow," said Sadie.

Shivon said, "Please find her for me!"

"All we can do is keep an eye out for her, Shivon," said Clarice as they moved down the steps toward their bikes. "Let us know if she comes home."

They pushed their bikes along the sidewalk. "What's this lead we're supposed to have, Number Two?" said Clarice.

"The pied piper, of course," said Sadie.

"Forget about the pied piper, Number Two. That's an order. Being trashed by skunks does not come under a detective's list of duties."

Sadie scowled.

"While we're here," said Clarice, "let's go tell Mrs. Reardon what the pest man said. Maybe she will know what to do about Rascal."

But Mrs. Reardon did not answer the harsh, grinding ring of her rusty doorbell.

Sadie pointed at her sensitive ears. "She's in the back," she said. "I can hear somebody banging about."

They trooped around to the back and Brick knocked on the kitchen door, which was slightly ajar.

"There's somebody inside," said Sadie. She stood on her toes, peeking in the window. She squealed with astonishment. "Raccoons!"

Clarice pushed the door open and they went inside.

A big raccoon was on the counter, sitting on its haunches, a box of corn flakes in front paws that were really more like tiny, dexterous hands.

Four baby raccoons were tumbling through the lower cupboards and skating about on a floor covered with flour, sugar, peanut butter, digestive biscuits, and honey spilled from a shattered jar.

The kitchen was a total mess.

The big raccoon, obviously the mother, was a salt-and-pepper colour, with beautiful white whiskers and a bushy black-and-white ringed tail. Her shoulders were stained blue with dye or paint. She was tearing at the cereal package with her sharp claws and poking her pointed snout inside to lick up the crumbs. Around her on the counter were spilled spices and flour, raisins and sugar, and the remains of a pot of strawberry jam.

The toaster and the kettle had fallen to the floor.

The three sleuths stood in the doorway, unable to advance without stepping into something unpleasant. The mother raccoon gave them hardly a glance. She abandoned the empty package and stood up on her hind feet to investigate the cupboards further, reaching in and pulling out bottles, cans, and jars which crashed to the counter and onto the stove or into the sink. A bottle of olive oil clattered to the floor and broke, scaring one of the babies and causing him to tumble backwards into the spilled honey.

Sadie heard a car door slam out front, then footsteps on the path outside. It was Mrs. Reardon carrying two heavy grocery bags. She came slowly up the back steps. "Oh, no!" she cried when she saw the mess. She dropped her shopping bags, grabbed a broom from the back step, and started to cross the kitchen floor after the mother raccoon, but stopped when she saw the broken glass and the quicksands of honey, jam and olive oil barring her way. "Get out of here!" she yelled.

The raccoons ignored her.

Mrs. Reardon began to cry.

Brick said, "Chrrhrrhrr!"

The mother raccoon immediately stopped investigating the upper shelves of the cupboard and crouched, all four feet on the counter, black glittering eyes staring through her bandit's mask at Brick.

Brick said, "Chrrhrr!"

Mother raccoon dropped to the floor and started a churring noise that sounded like the purr of a cat, but ten times louder. The four babies went to her quickly, slipping and sliding through the debris.

Brick said, "Chhchhrrhhhchrckhr," in a low throaty murmur that sounded much like the churr of the mother raccoon.

Stepping daintily past the four people in the doorway, the mother raccoon, her young ones behind her, loped and shuffled down the steps into the backyard. She sat on the grass and magnolia petals and waited in the spring sunshine, looking up at Brick, a patch of sky blue about her shoulders.

Brick said, "Chrrkkhrr."

The mother raccoon started licking the honey and jam and flour off her babies' soft fur.

Mrs. Reardon was speechless with astonishment.

Clarice said, "I've got a Hunch that these are the same raccoons Pete Packer took away."

Mrs. Reardon found her voice. "That's them

all right! No doubt about it. The mother's still got that blue paint on her back. She's come back for her missing baby, mark my words. Wait till I see that Pete Packer, just wait!"

"How did the mom get blue paint on her?" said Sadie.

"I was painting that little chair." Mrs. Reardon pointed to the blue chair on the porch rail. "It's the one my grandson Michael likes to sit on when he comes over with his mom for a visit — my eldest daughter, Darlene, lives up on Tenth — and I left the paint pot on the porch rail with the lid off. Momma raccoon reached up — raccoons are very curious creatures, you know — and pulled it down on herself. What a mess! Took me ages to clean the paint off the porch."

Sadie tiptoed down to yard level, unzipped her fanny pack, and placed the sleeping Rascal gently on the grass.

Mother raccoon gave a happy, excited, almost human cry. She lumbered forward and was all over Rascal, sniffing and licking and pawing and churring away like a washing machine. Rascal, still half asleep and floundering on his back, quickly recognized the sounds and smells of his birth, and squeaked with joy. The other four babies followed the mother, mewing and squealing and tumbling and rollicking about Rascal, delighted he was back. Rascal snuggled into his mother's belly, overjoyed to be home. Then the mother turned and shuffled off, her five kittens tripping and scrambling along behind her.

Sadie said sadly, "Goodbye, Rascal," as the baby raccoon disappeared under the porch with his family.

"Cheer up, Number Two," said Clarice. "Rascal's much better off now."

Sadie sighed. "I know."

Mrs. Reardon turned to Brick. "You're a very talented boy. It's almost like you *talked* to those raccoons."

Brick stared at her unblinkingly with his strange amber eyes under their yellow lashes.

"It's not only raccoons," said Sadie, "it's cats, dogs, lobsters, you name it. Brick was raised by lions in the jungle when his parents lost him, isn't that right, Brick?"

Brick said nothing; he merely yawned and scratched his spiky yellow head.

Sadie said, "His real name is Leopold Chumley-Smythe."

"Well, I never!" said Mrs. Reardon.

"Good work, Number Three," Clarice said to Brick.

"Thanks, Chief." Brick spoke very quietly, as though talking were an effort. His ears twitched like a cat's.

Clarice said, "What did Pete Packer tell you when he came to see you about moving the raccoons, Mrs. Reardon?"

"He said he could get rid of them for me. He gave me a choice. For twenty-five dollars he would chase them out from under the porch, and board up the hole so they couldn't get back in. Which meant they would have to find another home somewhere. Which would be cruel, I think. I didn't like the idea of just throwing them out, the mother nursing and all. What if they couldn't find another safe place?"

"What was the other choice?" asked Clarice.

"The only other choice was to pay a hundred and sixty-five dollars."

"Phew! That's a lot of money," said Clarice.

"It wasn't cheap, but he told me he'd take them to one of the designated areas for nuisance wildlife, as he called it — a nice place out in the forest, near the Squamish River, full of tasty, delicious crayfish, where the salmon come every year to spawn. A great place to raise young ones he said it was, far away from urban smog and harmful garbage-can menus." Mrs. Reardon shrugged and smiled. "He made it sound like a paradise. What else could I do?"

"That was very generous of you, Mrs. Reardon," said Sadie.

"I had a Hunch there was something phony about that pest control man," said Clarice.

"No you didn't," said Sadie. "It was me who spotted how phony he was."

Clarice said, "Those raccoons came back to Mrs. Reardon's place in under twenty-four hours. The Squamish River must be at least an hour's drive away from here. If Pete Packer took them there as he said he did, then they must have come back on the starship *Enterprise* at warp factor eight."

"What are you saying, Clarice?" said Sadie.

"I'm saying that rotten Pete Packer the pest man doesn't waste time and gas taking animals all the way out to the Squamish. He charges the top dollar but releases his animals right back into the neighbourhood, that's my Hunch."

"That's hardly a hunch, Clarice," said Sadie. "It's a simple deduction."

"Releasing animals in the neighbourhood makes more business for him," Clarice said to Mrs. Reardon.

"More business?" said Mrs. Reardon. "What do you mean?"

"If Pete Packer releases the animals in the neighbourhood," said Clarice, "and they get into somebody else's house or carport or under their porch, then the next thing is he'll be getting a call to come and take them away. Then he'll spin the story about the tasty crayfish and the salmon and the forest, and it's another one hundred and sixty-five bucks in his pocket. Simple."

Sadie said, "That's against the British Columbia Environment regulations. He could lose his licence."

"How do you know so much about environment regulations, Number Two?"

"I read them in the shop, remember?"

"Who would ever find out Pete broke the law?" said Clarice. "Unless he made a big mistake."

"Like leaving a baby behind," said Sadie.

"Right," said Clarice.

"Huk!" said Brick who had been following intently the relentless logic of his two colleagues in crime.

"But how do we prove it?" said Sadie.

"There's the blue paint," said Mrs. Reardon, who had also been following Clarice and Sadie's exchange, with a gleam in her eye.

"But what if Pete Packer denies there was blue paint on the animal he took away?" said Clarice. "It's your word against his, Mrs. Reardon. We need stronger proof than that."

"Well, Pete Packer isn't about to charge me twice," said Mrs. Reardon grimly. "I want you to take this case. If anyone can fix this dishonest pest control man it's the O'Brien Detective Agency!"

"My thoughts exactly," admitted Clarice modestly.

Chapter 8

The three detectives helped Mrs. Reardon clean up the broken glass and some of the other mess in her kitchen, and then they mounted their bicycles.

"We've got to Interview the Suspect and ask a few Searching Questions," announced Clarice.

They biked back to the Pied Piper shop.

Pete had his feet up, drinking a Coke. When he saw Brick coming he hurried around to the far side of the desk so that there was a good four feet of solid mahogany between him and the wild boy.

Clarice did not mince her words. "Mr. Packer.

You lied to us. You said you took Mrs. Reardon's raccoons out to Squamish. That wasn't true. All the animals are back under Mrs. Reardon's front porch again."

Sadie said, "What do you have to say for yourself?"

Pete looked nervously at Brick. "Under the porch? But how do you know it's the same family of raccoons?"

"That's easy, Mr. Packer," said Sadie. "The mother raccoon is blue from Mrs. Reardon's spilled paint. She recognized her immediately."

Pete smiled, showing his long yellow teeth. "The truth is, kids, I couldn't take them out to Squamish. I did the best I could, but it just didn't work out."

"What do you mean?" said Sadie.

"The van broke down just before I got to the Lions Gate Bridge. I got Tim Trodd's truck to tow me into the garage, but then Tim didn't have the parts to fix it right away, had to order them special the next day. I didn't want to keep the poor animals cooped up in their cages all night so I had to let 'em go. A humane act, you might say." He smiled sadly and placed a grimy hand on his heart.

"You could have saved us a lot of trouble," said Clarice, "and told us this yesterday. And shouldn't you have paid Mrs. Reardon her money back?"

"Haven't had time now, have I?" said Pete, his sad smile threatening to turn to tears and the hand clutching his chest jerking spasmodically.

"You must take the raccoons to Squamish as you promised," said Clarice.

"I will! I will!"

"Call Mrs. Reardon and make the arrangements," said Clarice.

"I will! I will!"

The three detectives mounted their bicycles and headed back to headquarters.

"I don't believe a word that man says," said Sadie in disgust as she picked up the shade card she had been working on earlier. "So what do we do now, Clarice?"

"Finish off these Canadian mohair cards and then tomorrow, if you feel like it, we can start on the Belgian cottons."

"About Pete Packer the pest man, I mean."

"He might be telling the truth about his van breaking down."

"Hmmph!" said Sadie.

"We'll just have to wait and see what he does when he gets his second chance," said Clarice. She got right down to work, deftly tying a green mohair sample. "If he dumps them in the neighbourhood again then we've got to catch him in the act. It's the only way. What he's doing isn't honest, and it isn't fair to people like Mrs. Reardon."

"It isn't fair to the raccoon family, either," said Sadie. "How would you like to be a little baby and lose your mom? Or be captured, caged and carted off to you know not where, with the helpless cries and screams of your little babies breaking your heart?"

"Chrrhrr," said Brick, settling down on the sacks.

"He's still talking to the raccoons," Sadie whispered. "Why not come and help with these cards, Number Three?" she said aloud.

Brick got up and stood beside her, watching.

"Are your hands clean?" said Sadie.

Brick showed his hands.

Sadie said, "You could sit on the stool at the corner of the desk."

Brick started helping himself to pieces of wool, the wrong colours.

Clarice stopped him. "Use the same colours as the sample on the wall, Number Three. Every shade card must be the same." She showed him her card. "There's a name beside each colour, see?" She pointed to the dark green. "That's called 'nottingham,' and this one is called 'sage.' The third green is called 'mint.' Get it?"

Brick frowned. "Right, Chief."

"We're out of nottingham green," Clarice said to Sadie. "Pass the scissors and I'll cut some more."

Sadie passed the scissors. "I'd love to see Rascal and his family find a good home," she said. "That place on the Squamish sounds so nice. No cars and buses, no smog, no noise, just miles and miles of open wilderness. The sounds of birds, the swift clean flow of the river, the salmon jumping—"

"Hold the other end of the skein while I cut it," said Clarice.

"—lots of grubs and minnows and crayfish and bird's eggs for them to eat; good, healthy wholesome natural food instead of slimy smelly leftovers in people's garbage cans." Sadie gave a long wistful sigh.

"Put all these in the nottingham green box," said Clarice, passing the short lengths of wool over to Sadie.

The two girls went back to their tying. Brick was absorbed in the work. The girls watched him. His fingers were already as fast as Clarice's and Sadie's.

Clarice said, "I've thought of a Plan."

"What plan?" said Sadie.

"The Simple Plan is always the Best Plan," said Clarice, flicking her titian hair from her eyes, suddenly all capitals and pomposity. "A good Detective goes right to the heart of the matter. I call it Focus. It's an important quality, the ability to Focus on the Problem and come up with a Simple Solution."

Sadie switched Clarice off and watched Brick's flying fingers. He was completing a card in half the time it took Sadie. She nudged Clarice. "Look."

Clarice looked. Her mouth dropped open.

Brick never failed to astonish them.

Clarice tore her eyes from Brick's flashing fingers. "Do you want to hear my Plan or not?"

"I have a feeling you'll tell us anyway."

Clarice said, "Here's the scenario: Mrs. Reardon calls the Perp to come over and take the raccoons away again, okay?"

"The perp?"

"Perpetrator. Police word for culprit, remember? Pete Packer the pest man is our Perp."

Sadie nodded, but with her attention divided between tying wool, Brick's amazing dexterity, and Clarice's alliterations and pompous capitals, she was having a hard time keeping up with what the chief detective was saying.

"So the Perp comes over to Mrs. Reardon's place," continued Clarice, "parks his wheels, and goes into the house or under the porch or whatever he does to capture the raccoons, okay?"

"Okay."

"That's when we jump into his van and hide."

"Hide in the perp's van," repeated Sadie, robot-like. Then she realized what Clarice was saying, "Are you crazy, Clarice? We can't do that!"

"Why not?"

"Rules, Clarice! Rules! We can't ride in a stranger's vehicle! Our parents would kill us!"

"Pete Packer is not a stranger. Besides, he's a weak old man. A robin's wing would bowl him over, and there's three of us and one of him. *And* he's terrified of Number Three. No, Number Two, I can't see any danger in riding with Pete Packer!"

"Maybe, but what if someone found out? And what if he's got other wild animals in the van — rats or skunks? I don't ever want to see another skunk as long as I live! Never!"

"Calm down, Number Two. If there are any other animals they'll be in cages. Now listen. We hide in the back of the van and see where he takes Mrs. Reardon's raccoons. If he takes them way out to the Squamish, fine. But if he releases them in the neighbourhood or in some other neighbourhood we've got him cold." Clarice smiled.

Sadie considered. "Maybe you're right, Clarice. I like the idea of reporting that lazy, greedy old man to the Environment Ministry. Which would be game over for Mr. Pete Packer the perfidious pest man." Now she was catching Clarice's alliteration disease.

"The Perp."

"Precisely."

"Case solved," agreed Clarice. "A piece of ca—"

"Pastry," said Sadie.

The girls reached for more cards, but Brick

had already completed and tossed the last one into the box under the desk and was lying down on the sacks, yawning and scratching. In five seconds he was fast asleep.

Chapter 9

The next morning when Sadie arrived at head-quarters she found the shed empty. She parked her bicycle and knocked on Clarice's back door.

"Hello, Sadie." Mrs. O'Brien smiled as she opened the door. "Come on in."

Mrs. O'Brien was an older edition of Clarice: same red hair, same serious green eyes, same stubborn chin. Sadie followed her in. "Thanks for all the work you did yesterday on the shade cards," she said. "It was an enormous help. Clarice said you and Brick are very good at it."

Sadie said, "I hope you get lots of orders."

Clarice and her dad were in the dining room working at the table. Clarice was inserting completed shade cards and price lists into grey O'Brien Yarn Company folders, and her father was sliding the folders into envelopes ready for mailing.

"Hi, Sadie," said Clarice.

"Good morning, Sadie," said Mr. O'Brien. He sounded happy.

"Would you like some breakfast, Sadie?" asked Mrs. O'Brien. "We've just had ours but there's lots left over."

"No thanks. I ate already."

"How about a glass of milk or juice?"

"No thanks, I'm fine."

"I can manage the rest, Clarice," said Mr. O'Brien. "You go off and play." Mr. O'Brien was dark and balding and had a nice smile.

"Play!" said Clarice indignantly. "We're not little kids! We don't *play*. We're Detectives, and we're working on a Case."

"What kind of case?" said Mr. O'Brien.

"Animals," said Clarice. "Raccoons mainly."

Mr. O'Brien laughed. "Now I understand why the skunk went after you both."

"Not funny, Daddy," said Clarice.

Mr. O'Brien became serious. "You're right, there's a veritable plague of skunks and raccoons this spring. I don't know where they're all coming from. Seems like I wake up every night with the backyard lights coming on. Burglars! I think, and I race to the window to look. Each time it's raccoons, or a skunk setting off the infra-red sensors!"

"We need a pied piper to lure them all away to the wilderness," said Sadie.

Mr. O'Brien nodded and smiled and began quoting from the Browning poem. " 'His queer long coat from heel to head/ Was half of yellow and half of red . . . ' "

Sadie continued, " 'And he himself was tall and thin, / With sharp blue eyes, each like a pin' ."

Mr. O'Brien laughed. "Well done, Sadie! Is your raccoon case like the plague of rats in the poem?"

"Not exactly—" Sadie began.

"It's secret and confidential," said Clarice, cutting her off. "We can't discuss the case with members of the public."

"Then go out and solve it," said Mr. O'Brien.

"Come on, Sadie." Clarice grabbed her jacket off the kitchen chair.

"Be careful out there," Mr. O'Brien yelled as they closed the door behind them.

As the girls stood on the small back porch pulling on their jackets, Brick arrived, swooping through the open gate and into the yard on his bicycle. He came to an abrupt stop a few centimetres from the side of the shed, slid from the saddle, and allowed the bike to park itself.

The girls stood a moment, admiring his cool athletic grace. Brick didn't notice the girls watching him. He opened the shed door. As he was poking his head inside the shed, a mouse ran out.

Brick turned in the wink of an eye and dived after the mouse. The mouse swerved, but Brick moved like greased lightning. Down on all fours, he swerved with the mouse, then somersaulted, landing in the mouse's path, his freckled nose close to the grass as though daring the tiny brown creature to run into his open mouth. The terrified mouse, seeing Brick's gleaming white teeth, dashed in the opposite direction, but Brick, a blur of yellow hair and blue jeans, whirled in a circle and was there before him. Again the mouse charged away, making for the safety of the long grass near the fence. Brick leaped like a cat and pinned the mouse's long tail between two fingers. The mouse was trapped.

Brick picked the mouse up gently around his tiny, fat belly, tickled his whiskers, then let him go, dropping him into the long grass where he disappeared in a flash.

The girls were speechless.

Brick looked up and saw them. He looked embarrassed. "Hi, Chief."

Still the girls stared. Clarice was the first to recover. "Say nothing," she whispered to Sadie out the side of her mouth. In as normal a voice as possible she said to Brick, "You're just in time, Number Three. Get back on your bike. We're heading out."

"Where to?" said Sadie, still in a bit of a daze.

"Mrs. Reardon called earlier. Wants to bring us up to date on Pete the pest man." Clarice pedalled out the gate and into the lane, Sadie and Brick behind her. They hurtled downhill in the bright sunshine, whizzed into Mrs. Reardon's front yard, dropped their bicycles on the ground under the last of the disintegrating magnolia goblets, and rang the rattling doorbell.

Mrs. Reardon poked her head out of an upstairs window, "Come in, dears. Door's open. I was expecting you."

They trooped in. Mrs. Reardon came down the stairs. The house smelled of pine-scented furniture polish. "Come through to the kitchen," she said. "It's all back to normal. Except for the toaster. It's broken. I'll have to buy a new one." The table was set with glasses and plates, a jug of orange juice, digestive biscuits, and a large cake. "I made you a nice chocolate cake for helping me with the clean-up yesterday. I don't know what I would have done without you."

"Chocolate," murmured Brick.

They all sat down. Mrs. Reardon poured juice and cut the cake, and the three friends went at it enthusiastically with their forks, two pieces each.

"There's one piece left over," said Mrs. Reardon some minutes later.

"I'm stuffed," said Sadie.

"No thanks," said Clarice.

The old lady pushed it toward Brick with a smile. Brick finished it off.

"My goodness!" said Mrs. Reardon happily.

"He's hollow," said Sadie. "If you tap him on the head it sounds like when you drop a stone into a deep well."

Mrs. Reardon laughed. "I don't believe you,"

she said. "Brick is the most solid boy I've met in many a long day."

They pushed back their chairs. Sadie took off her glasses and polished the lenses. Clarice wiped chocolate from her mouth. "That was a great chocolate cake, Mrs. Reardon. Thanks."

"Best I ever ate," said Sadie.

"Chocolate," murmured Brick contentedly.

"So what's the story on the Perp—Pete Packer, Mrs. Reardon?" asked Clarice.

"Oh, that man! He tried to give me a hard time, wanted to charge me again for taking those poor animals away, can you believe the cheek?" She shook her head. "He's not a bit like his brother, Patrick Packer — such a nice man — anyway, I gave him what-for. Reminded him about the blue paint on the mother's fur, and threatened to call the police. That did it. He promised to take them to where he should have taken them in the first place — the Squamish River."

"When?" asked Clarice.

"In about an hour, ten o'clock."

Clarice pursed her lips. "Are you certain the raccoons are still here?"

"Quite certain. They came up on the porch

last night and I gave the mother some sardines and an egg."

"Raccoons love sardines and eggs," said Sadie. "But you're not supposed to feed wild animals; it's not good for them."

"I know," said Mrs. Reardon, "but she *is* a mother with five babies to feed. And she *has* had a most traumatic time, losing her kitten and all. I figured she needs all the help she can get." The old lady sighed. "It would be so nice for my little raccoon family if that pest man would *really* take them to the wilderness."

"We have a plan, Mrs. Reardon," Clarice assured her. "We'll make sure Pete Packer keeps his promise. Just leave it to us!"

Chapter 10

Ten o'clock came and went.

By eleven, the waiting had worn Sadie down to the point where her sarcastic side was starting to get the better of her.

"You and your 'Best plan is the simplest plan,' Clarice! Simplest way to end up in the hospital, you mean! How can I read my book when my rear end is starting to rot and putrefy on this damp ground? I wouldn't be surprised if I end up with terminal bum decay. If I'd known we'd be hiding in a rhododendron bush for over an hour I'd have worn rubber underpants. And I don't know if you've noticed, Clarice, but there's a distinct skunk odor in here."

"Probably us," said Clarice.

The bush in which Clarice and Sadie were hiding was in Mrs. Reardon's backyard. It was almost dark inside the bush, and it was quite damp. Brick was hidden high and dry in an arbutus tree close by. The plan was that the three detectives would hide in Pete's van as soon as he parked and left it to go up to the house.

Sadie poked her head out of the thick leaves, her ears pointed in the direction of Sixth Avenue. She could see Brick's yellow head resting on a thick tree limb and one of his tattered sneakers hanging down through the leaves. His eyes were closed.

Sadie chewed the end of her hair.

"Pete Packer isn't punctual, Number Two."

"No, Clarice, he isn't. You might say that Pete Packer's punctuality is positively poor."

"Why won't you ever call me Chief, Number Two? I mean, we are on a Case, after all. Give me one good reason."

"I read in a book that you should never tell people your reasons for what you do."

"Why not?"

"Because your decision might be right, but your reasons are sure to be wrong."

Clarice shook her head as though to clear her ears. "Huh?"

"I hear something coming," said Sadie.

They waited. Soon Clarice could hear it too. She peered out. It was Pete Packer's white van lurching along the leafy back lane over the potholes. It came to a stop near the arbutus tree. They heard the slider door slam open and peered out at Pete's white-overalled back — with THE PEST MAN stencilled in red — as he reached into his van for equipment. They shrank back, waited, peeped out again and saw Pete walking up to the house carrying a very large cage in one hand and a long pole in the other. The pole was aluminum and had a noose at the end.

"The Perp's got a pole," whispered Clarice.

"Snare pole," Sadie whispered. "To catch the mother raccoon."

Pete's back disappeared around the corner of the house. "Now!" said Clarice, crashing out of the bush and leaping up to tug on Brick's sneaker. "Wake up, Number Three!"

The slider door was open. The three detectives jumped into the van and scrambled to the back, where they huddled together behind the stacks of empty cages. Except for the ones in the front, there were no windows in the van.

"Do you think he'll be able to see us?" whispered Sadie nervously.

"Sshhh!" said Clarice.

They waited.

"At least it's dry in here," whispered Sadie.

"Ssshhh!" said Clarice.

"I hear him," said Sadie. "He's coming back."

The pest man grunted as he lifted the heavy cage and slid it into the van. Then he threw the snare pole in after it and slammed the slider door shut. The pole rattled on the metal floor and came sliding back toward the detectives like a spear. The aluminum glittered, and Sadie could see that the wooden end-piece was scarred with tooth and claw marks, where scores of snared animals had fought for their freedom against the cruel bite of the wire cable. The wire cage was full of raccoons, and even in the dim light Sadie could see the blue paint-stain on the mother's shoulder and the frightened babies snuggling into her.

Pete Packer climbed into the van and started the engine.

Chapter 11

The van bumped and lurched down the lane, but once they reached the street the ride was smoother. They could see the back of Pete's head and not much else, but they didn't get very far, only to the shop. Pete drove round to the back, parked in the lane and got out, slamming the door shut behind him.

Sadie could see Clarice's green eyes staring back at her anxiously. Brick's eyes, however, were focused on the raccoons as he churred at them in friendly conversation. The mother seemed to relax under the drone of Brick's voice. Her babies snuggled into her, chittering and feeding.

"What do you think he'll say to us if he discovers us in his van?" said Sadie, worried.

Clarice clenched her jaw. "It's what *we* will say to *him* if he doesn't take these raccoons out to the Squamish!"

"What do you think he's doing now?" said Sadie.

Clarice shrugged.

"What if he stays here, Clarice, for two or three hours? We can't sit in this smelly old van all that time."

"We'll see."

They waited.

"Which one is Rascal?" Sadie asked Brick.

Brick thrust a finger into the cage and tickled a bushy little tail. The baby wriggled and pushed himself closer to his mother's belly.

"Hello, Rascal," Sadie whispered.

Brick churred away at the mother raccoon.

"Quiet! He's coming back!" said Sadie.

Pete Packer yanked the slider partly open, wide enough to allow him to push in two small cages containing squirrels, one black and the other grey. Then he slammed the door shut, threw himself into the driver's seat and restarted the engine. They were off once more. The squirrels chattered excitedly. Mother raccoon got up and gripped the cage wires with her paws, giving a loud keening cry that caused Pete to glance back. "Aaaw, shut up!"

Sadie and Clarice, afraid that Pete would see them, shrank back against the sides of the van, holding their breath. Mother raccoon lay down again, alert and agitated without the sound of Brick's consoling voice. Some of her babies began to cry.

The Squamish River was north. But Pete seemed to be heading south. He drove the van slowly along a bumpy lane and stopped. He switched off the engine, got out and opened the slider door. Sadie caught a glimpse of a vacant lot, screened from the neighbouring houses by a bank of wild blackberry bushes. Pete pulled the squirrel cages out onto the ground and opened them. The squirrels escaped into the bushes with little squeaks of joy. Pete threw the empty cages back into the van. Then he wrestled the raccoon cage out onto the ground. He was just about to open it when Clarice yelled, "Hold it right there, Mr. Packer!"

Pete looked up in surprise, his mouth opening and closing several times and his long, stained teeth chewing angrily at his lower lip. "What the—"

The detectives jumped down to the ground. They had Pete surrounded.

Pete moved away from Brick. "I'll have the police onto you kids for this," he yelled. "You got no right—"

"So go ahead and call the police," said Clarice. "But you won't, will you, Mr. Packer? Because what you're doing is illegal."

"We're witnesses," said Sadie. "We all saw you releasing trapped animals into the neighborhood instead of the wilderness. We've got you cold and you know it!"

Pete's little ice-blue eyes glittered angrily as he chewed his lip.

"Do you want your brother to lose his license?" asked Clarice.

At the mention of his brother Pete's face changed; he tried to smile, but the smile didn't quite work. The lips retreating from the stained teeth formed a trembling grimace. "Now look here, kids, you've got it all wrong. I wasn't freeing the raccoons here. No! I was merely checking the cage to be sure it was secure for the long trip up north. With all the bouncing about these cages get, the catch comes open sometimes, see?" He bent down and flicked at the catch with his finger to demonstrate how easily it opened. The mother raccoon snarled and tried to bite his finger, but Pete pulled it away in time.

"You're a lousy liar, Mr. Packer," said Clarice.

"Look, I don't harm the animals, do I? They'd just as soon be let go here as anyplace else."

"I read the Ministry regulations," said Sadie, "and you're licensed to live-trap *procyon lotor* so long as you—"

"Hey! I didn't trap any of these!" Pete protested.

"*Procyon lotor* is the scientific name for raccoons," said Sadie loftily. "You are allowed to trap them so long as you relocate them in the wilderness." She waved her arm toward the houses near the waste ground. "This is not the wilderness. It's an urban area in the city of Vancouver."

"Besides," said Clarice, "you charged Mrs. Reardon a hundred and sixty-five dollars to take them to the wilderness, remember? That's Embezzlement."

"Fraud." Sadie corrected her.

Brick waved his flattened hands slowly in front of his eyes. Pete paled and backed away.

"You've got to take them out to the Squamish River, Mr. Packer!" said Clarice. "Or else!"

Pete's face crumpled. "You got my solemn promise." He wet a finger and crossed his heart. "I'll take these little guys out to the Squamish if you think that's what they'd really like."

"That's what they would really like," said Sadie.

"And it's what Mrs. Reardon paid you to do," said Clarice.

Pete lifted the raccoon cage and swung it back into the van. "No problem. I'll have 'em there in a little over an hour."

"I don't trust him," whispered Sadie.

"We're coming with you," said Clarice, "to make sure you do the job properly."

Pete scowled. "That won't be necessary. I gave my word, didn't I?" But the detectives were already climbing back into the van. The girls made themselves comfortable by sitting in the rear seat and stretching out their legs. Brick sat up front with the pest man.

Pete cursed, slid the van door closed, climbed into his seat, and started the engine.

"You'll soon be in your new home, Rascal," said Sadie.

Pete, chewing his lips in vexation, drove quickly through downtown and over the Lions Gate Bridge to the White Spot restaurant in West Vancouver.

"Why are we stopping here?" said Clarice. "There's still an hour's drive ahead of us."

"Snack time," said Pete, turning in his seat. "Can't drive all the way to the Squamish River on an empty stomach." He smiled. "Come on, I'll buy you all a burger. Or anything you like. Food's on me."

Clarice said, "That's very generous of you, but we already had two slices—"

"Chocolate fudge brownie!" said Sadie excitedly. "White Spot makes the best!"

Clarice sighed. They went inside and ordered brownies. Pete had a burger. When he was almost finished, he wiped his mouth with his napkin and got up. "Be right back." He ambled off toward the washroom.

"This is great," said Sadie through a mouthful of brownie. "Maybe Pete isn't such a bad guy after all. At least he isn't mean with his money."

Clarice glanced out the window. "Hey! He's running to the van! The dirty Perp! Leaving us here! Quick! After him!" She jumped up, out of her seat.

Brick continued eating his brownie, not moving to let Sadie squeeze by him out of the booth. "Number Three!" yelled Sadie.

Brick reached into his jacket pocket and casually pulled out a bunch of keys.

Clarice and Sadie stared.

"Number Three, you picked Pete Packer's pocket!" said Sadie.

Brick shrugged.

"Well done, Number Three!" said Clarice. She took the keys and pocketed them.

Sadie plumped herself down again. "Well, really, Number Three, you might have said something."

They took their time finishing their chocolate fudge brownies.

Chapter 12

Pete Packer stomped angrily back into the restaurant.

Sadie looked up from her brownie and smiled sweetly at him. "Something the matter, Mr. Packer?"

Pete searched the table where he had been sitting, searched the seat, and then crawled about underneath the table. When he emerged his face was crimson.

"Looking for these?" Clarice shook the keys in front of his startled face.

Pete's crimson darkened to a violent purple. "Where did you find 'em?"

"Never mind that," said Clarice. "You were

trying to dump us so you could drive back to Vancouver and get rid of the raccoons there. But this time with no witnesses, right?"

Pete scowled. "I left my wallet in the van, that's all."

"What's that bulge in your hip pocket?" said Sadie. "Looks to me like it might be a wallet."

Pete pulled his wallet out, pretending surprise.

"We'll be outside," said Clarice, "while you're paying the bill."

They waited by the van. "That explains why he was so generous," said Sadie, "buying us lunch so he could get rid of us."

Pete came out of the White Spot. He was sulking. As he opened the door of the van an old yellow Chevy drove up and stopped with a squeal of brakes.

"He tried to ditch you. I saw him!"

The three detectives stared. "Mrs. Reardon!" Sadie exclaimed.

"I heard you talking while you were hiding in my bushes," said Mrs Reardon. "I figured he'd try something, so I followed."

She climbed out of the Chevy and looked at the sky. She was wearing a bright-pink jacket and a little red hat on top of her grey curls. "It's such a beautiful day." She turned to Clarice. "What do you say we take the raccoons ourselves?"

The detectives looked at each other. Then they looked at the trunk of Mrs. Reardon's car. Then they looked at Pete's scowling face.

"Why not?" said Clarice.

"Good idea!" said Sadie.

They lifted the raccoon cage into the trunk of the Chevy.

"Hello, Rascal," said Sadie. "I brought something for your mom." Sadie opened a paper napkin and pushed a piece of chocolate brownie through the wire mesh. The mother sniffed at it, rolled it around in her paws, then gobbled it down.

Pete climbed into his van.

"Thanks for a great lunch, Mr. Packer," said Clarice.

"You owe me one-forty, Pete Packer!" said Mrs. Reardon. "Just be sure I get it."

"Kids today!" Pete growled as he drove off, back to Vancouver. The detectives piled into the Chevy and Mrs. Reardon drove north through West Vancouver and Lions Bay. Soon they were bowling along the Highway on the edge of Howe Sound. Below them, sport fishermen trolled for salmon from their boats along the edges of the cliffs, while up ahead the sun glittered brightly on snow-capped Mount Garabaldi and the jagged peaks of the Tantalus Range.

Sadie studied Mrs. Reardon's map. The ride was smooth for almost an hour, until they crossed a bridge over the Squamish River.

"Turn left here," said Sadie.

Mrs. Reardon turned onto a bumpy gravel road and followed the Squamish for a few miles, then came to a stop at the end of the road.

They all got out of the car. Mrs. Reardon opened the trunk.

The mother raccoon, as though sensing the importance of this stop, began to make excited grunting noises. "We're here," Sadie announced to the raccoons. "We're in your new country!"

The detectives stretched their cramped limbs and looked about them. They were in the Squamish Valley, surrounded by forest and mountains and sky. A few metres away the river, swollen by the spring run-off, raced and splashed its way to the sea.

Sadie took a deep breath and stretched her arms to the sky. "Mmmm!"

"Beautiful!" murmured Clarice.

Brick, lithe and skinny, leaped like a mountain goat on boulders at the river's edge. "Aieee!" he cried, waving his arms about, hands chopping the bright clear air.

When they had finished stretching and jumping they lifted the cage out of the trunk and down onto the ground. They stood back. Brick squatted beside the cage and talked to the mother raccoon.

"Chhhrr," he said.

"Cchhkkrr," said the blue raccoon, her eyes gleaming with excitement.

Brick released the catch on the cage door and stood back. The blue raccoon emerged cautiously, sniffing the air suspiciously. She crouched in the grass and wildflowers at the edge of the gravel road, looking about her. When she was satisfied that there was no danger she called to her babies and they followed her quickly to the safety of the salal bushes near the forest boundary.

"Goodbye, Rascal," Sadie called at her last sight of the raccoons before they were gone for ever. "Goodbye." She wanted to cry.

She felt Clarice's hand in hers.

Mother raccoon stopped, sat upright on her haunches, and looked back. Sadie and Clarice waved. Then the mother raccoon, her babies tripping about her feet, entered the forest. The last thing to disappear from view was the patch of sky blue on her shoulder.

Brick stood silently on a boulder, hands thrust deep in his pockets, watching.

Mrs. Reardon dabbed at her eyes with a tiny handkerchief. "I'm so happy for them."

They all stood for a while watching a pair of eagles circling lazily high above the pines in the rising air.

"I hope Rascal will be safe," said Sadie.

"The mother is strong and clever," said Mrs. Reardon. "She will protect her little ones, you can be sure of that."

They got back in the Chevy. Sadie climbed in last beside Mrs. Reardon. "I wish I could stay here," she said, "it's so beautiful. I wish I was a raccoon living in a forest."

Clarice said, "Where will they go, I wonder?"

Sadie said, "They'll soon find a den. In an old hollow tree probably, where they'll be warm in the winter."

"Chhrr," murmured Brick in the back seat.

"Pete Packer is not an honest man," said Sadie. "Animals have got to be treated properly. Some people think that because we're smarter than animals, we're better. Well, we're not better. Animals have got rights, the same as you and me."

"You're quite right, Sadie," said Mrs. Reardon.

She started the engine and they headed for home.

* * *

"I'm delighted the wee things finally made it to the river," said Mrs. Reardon happily when they got back home. "You all did a wonderful job." She reached into her purse. "I'll be sure to recommend the O'Brien Detective Agency to any of my friends who have problems." She handed some folded bills to Clarice.

"Thanks, Mrs. Reardon," said Clarice, stuffing the money into her jeans pocket. "I hope you get back the money you paid to Pete Packer."

"Don't you worry about that. I will get it all right. And I intend to tell his brother Patrick everything that's happened when he gets back from his holiday. Pete must never be left in charge again."

Chapter 13

"Let's go celebrate the raccoon case wrap-up at the fudge shop," said Clarice as they jumped on their bicycles.

"Butterscotch," said Sadie.

"Maple," said Clarice.

"Chocolate ripple," murmured Brick.

They careened down the hill to False Creek, raced along the seawall and across the tiny wooden bridge onto Granville Island, then swooped between the Waterfront Theatre and Kids Only Market; rattled along the boardwalk at Brokers Bay, pedalled furiously past the sailboats and motor cruisers, zigzagged through the boat yard, and finally came to a stop riding their front wheels into the bicycle rack. When the fluttering, indignant pigeons outside Granville Market had settled themselves, it seemed to Sadie that they all stood facing the sound of music. "The pied piper!" she exclaimed.

The piper was playing in the triangular area adjacent to the bakery shop. The detectives joined the crowd of people who sat listening and eating pastries on the wooden benches which formed the triangle's boundaries. There were several families with children, a couple of dogs, a cat, a Canada goose, and a flock of starlings, the latter perched on the roof of the bakery.

After a few minutes, the piper stopped playing. He picked up his bowl, overflowing with coins and bills, and emptied its contents into the Animal Rights collection box on the bakery counter.

"Well! Just look at that!" said Sadie.

The piper emerged from the bakery and headed toward the market. He stopped when he saw Clarice and Sadie.

"Hello," he said. "Aren't you the two girls who got skunked on Friday?" His piercing blue eyes glittered merrily.

"So?" said Sadie, suspicious.

But the piper wasn't about to make fun of them. Instead, he removed his coloured hat with the long peacock feather, and gave a deep bow. "Allow me to tender my most abject apologies," he said. "It was very impolite of me to have laughed. But you both looked so funny, I couldn't help myself. I humbly apologize for my inexcusable manners."

Sadie smiled. A nice man, after all.

Clarice moved on the wooden bench to make room for the piper to sit.

"I hope," said the piper as he took a seat beside Clarice, "that the scrubbing wasn't too painful." He placed his flute across his knees. Sadie noticed that the backs of his hands were marked with several long scars that ran from fingers to wrists.

"We had to burn our clothes," said Clarice.

"Tut, tut! That's too bad," said the piper sympathetically. "But there isn't much else one can do with apparel thus savaged by our furry but stinky friends."

"Would you happen to have seen a black-and-white rabbit named Betsy?" said Sadie. "We've looked everywhere for her."

"Rabbit? Black-and-white? Hmmmn. I

might have seen one around here somewhere."
The piper put his pipe to his lips and played
a hippity-hoppity tune.

Around the corner came a rabbit, who began
nibbling daintily at a clump of narcissi outside
the bakery. Her shiny fur was black and white.

"Look!" said Sadie, "It's Betsy!"

The rabbit nibbled contentedly in the magical
aura of the piper's music, while beside her a
tabby cat performed her ablutions with graceful
licks and swipes at her fur.

"Go get her, Number Three," said Clarice.

But Brick seemed hypnotized by the piper's
music. His amber eyes were glazed and staring.

Sadie glided over, scooped the rabbit up grace-
fully, and clasped her to her chest. "Got long ears
all right. Must be the right one." She stroked the
furry bundle and sat down beside the piper.

"You must be the real Pied Piper," she said,
"the one who got rid of all the rats in Hamelin
town by the River Weser deep and wide."

The merry musician smiled. "Of course! 'Poor
piper as I am/in Tartary I freed the Cham/last
June from his huge swarm of gnats'."

" 'And eased in Asia, the Nizam/of a mon-
strous brood of vampire bats'?" asked Sadie.

"That's right!"

"Then you *are* the real Pied Piper," said Sadie happily.

"No, he's not," said Clarice. "His name is Patrick Packer and he owns a pest control business." She turned to the piper. "And for your information, Mr. Packer, your brother is making a real mess of things while you're out enjoying yourself pretending to be someone you're not."

The piper groaned. "Don't tell me that Pete has been up to his old tricks again! Has he been stuffing squirrels into people's basements?"

"Not exactly," said Clarice.

"Releasing rats into people's attics?"

Clarice shook her head.

"Mice?"

"Much worse," said Clarice. "He lied to old Mrs. Reardon and overcharged her."

"Dear, dear!" moaned Patrick Packer. "That's the last straw. I've warned him often enough. Tomorrow I will have to fire him."

"Serves him right," said Sadie.

Patrick Packer got up. "Goodbye," he said. "Come visit me at the Pied Piper shop when you get a chance."

"We would like that," said Sadie.

Clarice looked at her watch. "Let's go get that fudge before the market closes," she said.

Chapter 14

They hurried toward the market entrance.

"But what about Betsy?" Sadie jerked her chin at the sign on the door. "Animals are not allowed in the market."

"Bring her along," said Clarice. "Just keep her in your jacket. Nobody will know."

Sadie slipped the rabbit into the front of her jacket and peered in to make sure that she was comfortable.

"Come on," said Clarice, leading the way.

A bored Doberman, its lead tied to the bicycle stand, twitched his nose at Sadie's illegal cargo, then jumped up on her and gave a friendly "Wuff." Sadie thought she was hearing an unfriendly growl and leaped back in alarm. The frightened rabbit tumbled out of her jacket, hopped through the open market door, and disappeared into the crowd of shoppers.

"After her!" yelled Sadie.

The three detectives threw themselves into the crowd. Shoppers scattered in confusion.

"Look, Mummy!" yelled a little girl. "It's the Easter bunny!" The detectives chased the rabbit through the market, past the butcher, the baker, the Easter-egg maker, past the pasta shop and the filbert stall and the man who made the masks and puppets and walking birds, and ran right into the fudge shop.

"You can't come in here!" cried the assistant, the thin young woman with glasses.

"Get out!" shouted the fudge man over his shoulder. He was pouring warm butterscotch fudge from a big copper kettle onto a huge marble-topped table. The rabbit darted between his legs seeking a hiding place. The fudge man stumbled.

Butterscotch fudge spilled from the kettle onto the floor and onto Betsy, who was instantly trapped like a fly on flypaper. She couldn't move a whisker.

"I've got her!" yelled Sadie, pouncing on the butterscotched bunny.

Roaring with anger, the fudge man fell over her. The kettle flew from his hands, sending splashes of fudge everywhere.

"Let's go," said Clarice.

"Sorry!" Sadie said to the fudge man's assistant. She led the way from the shop like Joan of Arc, Betsy raised high like a banner in front of her.

They ran quickly through the aisles of vegetables and fruit, through the flower shop and out to their bicycles. The pigeons muttered, "Excuse me, excuse me," as they fluttered out of the way.

"I can't carry Betsy like this!" Sadie held the sticky rabbit up in the air.

"Here," said Clarice, "use this." She picked up a plastic bag and held it open while Sadie lowered Betsy into it and wrapped it about the shivering animal, leaving the end open for her nose. Then Sadie stuffed Betsy into her jacket.

They mounted their bicycles and headed for Shivon's. "I was right," said Sadie. "I told you so, Clarice! Betsy was lured by the pied piper!"

"It was just a coincidence," said Clarice.

Shivon clapped her hands in delight when

she saw her furry pet. "You found her!" she cried.

"Sorry about the fudge," said Sadie, handing the sticky rabbit over to her mistress.

"And it might be an idea to get Betsy a proper hutch," said Clarice.

Shivon laughed happily and kissed Betsy's sticky nose. "Thanks for bringing her back to me." She leaned down, opened a drawer in a small hallway table, and took out three bars of chocolate which she handed to Clarice. "Your Robin Hoods."

Clarice slipped them into her pocket with a nod.

"You're the greatest detectives ever," said Shivon.

"We do the best we can," said Clarice.

* * *

The next day was Tuesday and it was back to school for the three friends.

Clarice and Sadie called on Mrs. Reardon on the way home.

"Did Pied Piper return your money, Mrs. Reardon?" asked Clarice.

"Yes, indeed! Patrick insisted I take a full refund. Then he closed up the hole under the porch so no other animals can get in, and gave me a free voucher for next time, if there is a next time." She smiled happily. "Would you like to come in for a cup of tea?"

"No thanks," said Clarice. "We just wanted to make sure everything was wrapped up."

After supper, the detectives met again in the O'Brien potting shed.

"That was a great holiday weekend!" said Clarice.

Sadie, slumped in the client chair, sighed wistfully. "I wonder what Rascal is doing right now."

"Sleeping, probably. Raccoons are knock-turner, remember?"

"Nocturnal," Sadie corrected her. "I miss him. But I'm glad he's free and that he'll grow up in the wilderness."

Clarice leaned back in her chair, arms clasped behind her head. "Another Case solved."

Brick was already drowsing on the potato sacks after a hard day under the eye of his teacher, Miss Rogers, who firmly discouraged relaxation and sleep. He murmured, "Right, Chief."

"Two cases if you include Betsy," said Sadie.

Clarice nodded. "Two Cases in one, you might

say; the rabbit Case led to the raccoon Case, and we managed to solve both."

"We would have solved the rabbit case much sooner if you'd listened to my pied piper theory."

"Write up your report like it's all the one Case," said Clarice.

Sadie took off her glasses and started cleaning them with her little square of cloth. "I'll call it The Pied Piper Mystery."

"No," said Clarice. "There was no mystery to the pied piper. He was just funny old Patrick Packer taking a holiday, living in a make-believe world for a long weekend."

"Well, I think Patrick Packer *is* the real Pied Piper," said Sadie. "Anyway, how did you know the Pied Piper was Patrick Packer?"

Clarice yawned. "I didn't really. I just played a Hutch—"

"Hunch."

"That's what I said, a Hunch. I noticed that the backs of his hands were scarred, just like his brother's. The scars come from handling wild animals. And besides, the two brothers look alike, same shape, same receding chin, same piercing blue eyes. Clean Pete up, take away a few years and add some hair, clean teeth and a nice personality, and he'd be just like Patrick Packer. Another thing was what Mrs. Reardon said. Patrick was away on one of his crazy holidays, remember? I didn't think anything of it at the time, but later I just put it all together."

"I knew there was something familiar about Pete," said Sadie. She thought for a minute. "Another reason I think Patrick Packer is the real Pied Piper is the unusual numbers of raccoons and skunks this spring. You heard your dad and Mrs. Reardon. A *plague* of them, they said! It's simply too much of a coincidence."

Clarice sighed patiently. "Pied piper or no pied piper, the biggest part of the weekend was proving that Pete Packer was a cheat. When you write your report, call it 'The Case of the Blue Raccoon.' "

"I'm the secretary," said Sadie loftily. "I'll call it 'The Mystery of the Pied Piper.' "

"I'm the Chief Detective and I make all the Important Decisions. Call it 'The Case of the Blue Raccoon.' "

"I think we ought to take turns at being Chief Detective," complained Sadie. "It's only fair."

Brick murmured in his sleep, "Right, Chief."

Sadie smiled sweetly. "There, you see? Number Three called me Chief!" She yawned and stretched her arms over her head. "Goodnight, Rascal," she called to the ceiling, "wherever you are."

James Heneghan is a retired school teacher —
and a former police officer, fingerprint expert
and photographer. Whether in the classroom or
on the streets, his experience in crime gives him
lots of ideas for mystery writing!

James has written several novels for young
readers, including *Blue, Promises to Come, Torn
Away* and, of course, the rest of the O'Brien
Detective Agency series. He lives in Vancouver,
British Columbia.